ON LINE

J 641.539
Schwa
Schwartz, Heather E.

**Banana Split Pizza and Other
Snack Recipes**

Fun Food for Cool Cooks

Banana Split Pizza

AND OTHER SNACK RECIPES

by Heather E. Schwartz

Capstone
press®

Mankato, Minnesota

Snap Books are published by Capstone Press,
151 Good Counsel Drive, P.O. Box 669, Mankato, Minnesota 56002.
www.capstonepress.com

Library of Congress Cataloging-in-Publication Data
Schwartz, Heather E.
    Banana split pizza and other snack recipes / by Heather E. Schwartz.
    p. cm. — (Snap books. Fun food for cool cooks)
    Summary: "Provides fun and unique recipes to serve for snacks, including cookies, salads, and dips.
Includes easy instructions and a helpful tools glossary with photos" — Provided by publisher.
    Includes bibliographical references and index.
    ISBN-13: 978-1-4296-1339-2 (hardcover)
    ISBN-10: 1-4296-1339-4 (hardcover)
    1. Snack foods — Juvenile literature. 2. Cookery — Juvenile literature. I. Title. II. Series.
TX740.S32583 2008
641.5'3 — dc22   2007028314

Editor: Christine Peterson
Designer: Juliette Peters
Photo Stylist: Kelly Garvin

Photo Credits:
All principle photography in this book by Capstone Press/Karon Dubke
Capstone Press/TJ Thoraldson Digital Photography, cooking utensils (all)
Hot Shots Photo, 32

Capstone Press thanks Dino's Pizzeria in North Mankato, Minnesota, for assisting with photo shoots
for this book.

1 2 3 4 5 6 13 12 11 10 09 08

14/01/08
SB
$18.95

TABLE OF CONTENTS

PAGE 10

PAGE 14

PAGE 16

PAGE 22

PAGE 24

PAGE 26

INTRODUCTION

SEEING STARS!

When choosing a recipe, let the stars be your guide. Just follow this chart to find recipes that fit your cooking comfort level.

EASY: ★ ☆ ☆

MEDIUM: ★ ★ ☆

ADVANCED: ★ ★ ★

You've just arrived home from a long day at school. It's hours until dinner, but you've got that familiar rumble in your stomach. You're hungry! Now is the perfect time for a snack. The old standbys — potato chips, popcorn, a frozen burrito — just won't do. You need something more original to satisfy your cravings.

That's where this book comes in, with plenty of easy recipes you can make and eat between meals. These recipes are perfect for a tasty late-night snack or party treat. Stake your claim to the kitchen, and gather your tools and ingredients. It's time to give your taste buds a treat.

METRIC CONVERSION GUIDE

United States	Metric
¼ teaspoon	1.2 mL
½ teaspoon	2.5 mL
1 teaspoon	5 mL
1 tablespoon	15 mL
¼ cup	60 mL
⅓ cup	80 mL
½ cup	120 mL
⅔ cup	160 mL
¾ cup	175 mL
1 cup	240 mL
1 quart	1 liter

United States	Metric
1 ounce	30 grams
2 ounces	55 grams
4 ounces	110 grams
½ pound	225 grams
1 pound	455 grams

Fahrenheit	Celsius
325°	160°
350°	180°
375°	190°
400°	200°
425°	220°
450°	230°

All good cooks know that a successful recipe takes a little preparation. Use this handy checklist to save time when working in the kitchen.

BEFORE YOU BEGIN

READ YOUR RECIPE

Once you've chosen a recipe, carefully read over it. The recipe will go smoothly if you understand the steps and techniques.

CHECK THE PANTRY

Make sure you have all the ingredients on hand. After all, it's hard to bake cookies without sugar!

DRESS FOR SUCCESS

Wear an apron to keep your clothes clean. Roll up long sleeves. Tie long hair back so it doesn't get in your way — or in the food.

GET OUT YOUR TOOLS

Sort through the cupboards and gather all the tools you'll need to prepare the recipe. Can't tell a spatula from a mixing spoon? No problem. Refer to the handy tools glossary in this book.

PREPARE YOUR INGREDIENTS

A little prep time at the start will pay off in the end.

- Rinse any fresh ingredients such as fruit and vegetables.
- Use a peeler to remove the peel from foods like apples and carrots.
- Cut up fresh ingredients as called for in the recipe. Keep an adult nearby when using a knife to cut or chop food.
- Measure all the ingredients and place them in separate bowls or containers so they're ready to use. Remember to use the correct measuring cups for dry and wet ingredients.

PREHEAT THE OVEN

If you're baking treats, it's important to preheat the oven. Cakes, cookies, and breads bake better in an oven that's heated to the correct temperature.

The kitchen may be unfamiliar turf for many young chefs. Here's a list of trusty tips to help you keep safe in the kitchen:

KITCHEN SAFETY

ADULT HELPERS

Ask an adult to help. Whether you're chopping, mixing, or baking, you'll want an adult nearby to lend a hand or answer questions.

FIRST AID

Keep a first aid kit handy in the kitchen, just in case you have an accident. A basic first aid kit contains bandages, a cream or spray to treat burns, alcohol wipes, gauze, and a small scissors.

WASH UP

Before starting any recipe, make sure to wash your hands. Wash your hands again after working with other messy ingredients like jelly or syrup.

HANDLE HABITS

Turn handles of cooking pots toward the center of the stove. You don't want anyone to bump into a handle that's sticking off the stove.

USING KNIVES

It's always best to get an adult's help when using knives. Choose a knife that's the right size for both your hands and the food. Hold the handle firmly when cutting, and keep your fingers away from the blade.

COVER UP

Always wear oven mitts or use pot holders to take hot trays and pans out of the oven.

KEEP IT CLEAN

Spills and drips are bound to happen in the kitchen. Wipe up messes with a paper towel or a clean kitchen towel to keep your workspace clean.

Tell friends about this recipe, and they'll think you're topping a regular pizza with bananas. Yuck! Keep them guessing until they bite into the rich chocolate crust. Yum!

DIFFICULTY LEVEL: ★ ★ ☆
SERVING SIZE: 6
PREHEAT OVEN: 375° FAHRENHEIT

BANANA SPLIT PIZZA

WHAT YOU NEED

•• *Ingredients*

1 package brownie mix
2 (8-ounce) packages of
  cream cheese, softened
⅔ cup powdered sugar
1 cup sliced bananas
1 (8-ounce) can crushed pineapple,
  drained
1 cup sliced fresh strawberries
¼ cup semi-sweet chocolate chips

•• *Tools*

mixing bowl

pizza pan

electric mixer

rubber scraper

nonstick cooking spray

1 Mix brownie batter in a mixing bowl according to package directions.

2 Cover a pizza pan with a thin coating of nonstick cooking spray. Pour brownie batter onto the pan and bake for 15 to 20 minutes until firm.

3 Remove pizza pan from oven with oven mitts or pot holders. Set brownies aside to cool.

4 Place cream cheese and powdered sugar in a mixing bowl. Using an electric mixer at medium speed, blend ingredients until smooth. Spread on the brownie crust with a rubber scraper.

5 Top pizza with drained bananas, pineapple, and sliced strawberries.

6 Sprinkle chocolate chips on top of pizza. Chill pizza before serving.

Variation

Try topping the pizza with melted chocolate. Add chocolate chips and 1 tablespoon butter or margarine to a saucepan. Cook over medium heat, stirring until smooth. Cool mixture slightly. Drizzle warm chocolate over pizza.

History of the Banana Split

Two towns claim to be the home of the banana split. Residents of Latrobe, Pennsylvania, say the banana split was first served at the Tassell Pharmacy in 1904. But residents in Wilmington, Ohio, claim a local restaurant owner invented this treat in 1907.

Serve these cookies to an adult crowd, and they'll be amazed at your baking skills. Everyone knows stained glass is pretty, but who knew it was good enough to eat?

DIFFICULTY LEVEL: ★ ★ ★
SERVING SIZE: 6
PREHEAT OVEN: 375° FAHRENHEIT

STAINED-GLASS COOKIES

WHAT YOU NEED

●● *Ingredients*

⅓ cup vegetable shortening
1 egg
⅓ cup sugar
3 cups sifted, all-purpose flour
½ teaspoon baking soda
1 teaspoon salt
⅔ cup honey
1 (13-ounce) bag of LifeSavers

●● *Tools*

mixing bowl   electric mixer   small mixing bowl

 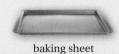

rolling pin   baking sheet

zip-top plastic bag
parchment paper

1 Place vegetable shortening in a mixing bowl. Use an electric mixer on medium speed to cream the shortening until smooth.

2 Crack an egg into a small mixing bowl and pour egg into the creamed vegetable shortening.

3 Add sugar, flour, baking soda, salt, and honey to the mixture. Mix with electric mixer until smooth. Chill dough in refrigerator for one hour.

4 Put each candy color into a separate zip-top plastic bag and close tightly. Crush the candies with a rolling pin.

5 Place dough on a floured surface. Roll out small handfuls of dough into snake-like strips about ¼ inch thick and 10 inches long.

6 Cover a baking sheet with parchment paper. On the baking sheet, form the dough strips into simple shapes, like circles or squares. Fill centers of cookies with crushed candy. Bake for 8 to 10 minutes.

10

Chill Out!

You've just finished making a batch of cookie dough. Time to pop them in the oven, right? Not quite. Most cookie doughs need to chill in the refrigerator for an hour or longer. Chilled dough is firmer and easier to work with than dough that's warm or at room temperature.

Fun Fact

A chocolate maker named Clarence Crane invented LifeSavers in 1912. LifeSavers got their name because Crane thought the candy looked like tiny life preservers.

Remember — Always wear oven mitts or use pot holders when taking trays or pans out of the oven.

This tempting snack looks like French fries, but don't be fooled. You won't want to serve them with ketchup. Serve these sweet fries during a movie night with friends.

"NUT" REALLY FRIES

WHAT YOU NEED

●● Ingredients

1 cup sweetened condensed milk
10-ounce package peanut
    butter chips
1 small tube red icing

●● Tools

microwave-safe
mixing bowl

rubber scraper

square baking pan

cutting board

sharp knife

aluminum foil
nonstick cooking spray

1 Combine milk and peanut butter chips in a microwave-safe bowl.

2 Melt mixture in microwave for about 2 minutes. Stop and stir the mixture with a rubber scraper every 30 seconds until smooth.

3 Line a 9-inch square baking pan with aluminum foil. Spray the foil with nonstick cooking spray.

4 Pour the mixture into the pan and cool completely at room temperature until firm.

5 Remove the mixture by tipping the pan upside down on a cutting board. It should come out in one big piece with the foil stuck to the top.

6 Peel off the foil. Using a sharp knife, slice the mixture into strips about 3 inches long and ¼ inch wide.

7 Drizzle red icing on top of the fries and serve.

French Fry Fake Out

You can make this snack look even more like fries from your favorite restaurant. Just fold a paper baking cup in half and set it on a plate. Fill the liner with about 10 fries. Place the fries so they pop out the top.

Chances are you've accidentally eaten sand while sunning on the beach. While real sand doesn't taste good, this yummy treat does. Serve this sand and watch everyone dig in.

DIFFICULTY LEVEL: ★ ★ ☆
SERVING SIZE: 6

SWEET SAND

WHAT YOU NEED

●● *Ingredients*

1 8-ounce package vanilla wafers
1 3-ounce package instant
    vanilla pudding
3 ½ cups prepared whipped
    topping, thawed
1 4.5-ounce package gummy fish

●● *Tools*

rolling pin

mixing bowl

mixing spoon

rubber scraper

zip-top plastic bag
small plastic cups

1 Put vanilla wafers in a zip-top plastic bag and secure it tightly. Crush vanilla wafers with a rolling pin.

2 Using a mixing bowl and large spoon, prepare pudding according to directions on the box.

3 Using a rubber scraper, fold whipped topping and half of the crushed cookies into the pudding.

4 Using the same rubber scraper, fold gummy fish into the pudding mixture. Save a few fish to decorate the top layer of your cups.

5 Spoon a layer of the remaining crushed wafers into plastic cups. Save some cookies for the topping. Each cup should be about ⅓ full.

6 Add a layer of the pudding mixture to each cup. Then top each cup with crushed wafers and gummy fish.

7 Chill the cups of Sweet Sand for one hour in the refrigerator.

How to Fold Your Food

Folding is a delicate mixing skill that doesn't call for stirring. Ingredients are gently blended together. Add the lighter ingredient to the heavier mixture. Then, slice into both with a rubber scraper. Gently lift some of the heavier mixture from the bottom. Fold the heavy mixture over the top of the lighter ingredient.

15

Pizza is popular at any party, but ordering in seems so ordinary. Want something different? Try this tasty pizza snack. It's made in a pot instead of a pan.

DIFFICULTY LEVEL: ★ ★ ☆
SERVING SIZE: 6

FUN PIZZA FONDUE

WHAT YOU NEED

● ● *Ingredients*

1 (29-ounce) jar of meatless
    spaghetti sauce
1 (8-ounce) package of shredded
    mozzarella cheese
¼ cup grated Parmesan cheese
2 teaspoons oregano
1 teaspoon Italian seasoning
1 teaspoon minced onion
¼ teaspoon garlic salt
¼ teaspoon black pepper
1 loaf Italian bread

● ● *Tools*

fondue pot

measuring spoons

mixing spoon

fondue forks

1 Place spaghetti sauce and cheeses into a fondue pot.

2 Use measuring spoons to measure seasonings. Add seasoning to spaghetti sauce mixture and stir with a mixing spoon.

3 Heat on medium. Stir ingredients with the mixing spoon until the cheeses are melted.

4 Tear bread into bite-sized chunks about 1 inch thick.

5 Use fondue forks to dip bread into the pot of pizza fondue.

Fondue Manners

Use your fondue fork to dip, but don't put this fork in your mouth. You don't want to double-dip in a shared pot. That could spread germs. Yuck! After you dip, slide the bread off your fork and onto your own clean plate.

Trusty Tip

Don't own a fondue pot? Just use a slow cooker to make this dip. Combine all of the ingredients in a slow cooker. Heat the dip on a high setting until warm. Use wooden skewers instead of fondue forks for dipping.

Lettuce, tomatoes, and carrots. How boring! Try this twist on basic salad ingredients. You'll never think of salads as boring again!

DIFFICULTY LEVEL: ★ ☆ ☆
SERVING SIZE: 1

KID SALAD

WHAT YOU NEED

●● *Ingredients*

1 egg
1 head lettuce
1 tomato
celery sticks
1 carrot
raisins
1 stick string cheese

●● *Tools*

saucepan

cutting board

sharp knife

vegetable peeler

salad plate

1 Hard-boil an egg in a small saucepan over high heat. (See instructions on page 19.)

2 Tear off a large lettuce leaf and place it on a plate. On a cutting board, slice the tomato in half lengthwise with a sharp knife. Place the tomato on top of the lettuce.

3 Cut celery into small sticks. Arrange celery sticks around the tomato as arms and legs.

4 With a vegetable peeler, remove peel from carrot. Slice one round chunk from the center of a carrot. Then, slice the round chunk in half. Place the two carrot pieces at the bottom of the celery stick legs.

5 Peel the hard-boiled egg and slice into round circles. Place one circle at the top of the tomato to create a head.

6 Create a face using raisins as eyes and nose. Slice a small piece of tomato for the mouth.

7 Use long strips of string cheese to make hair.

Hard-Boiled How-To

1 Place egg in a small saucepan and add cold water until the egg is completely covered.

2 Heat over high heat until water begins to boil.

3 Cook egg in boiling water for 10 more minutes.

4 Remove egg from the pan. Place it into a bowl of ice water until cool.

5 To peel the egg, gently crack the shell on all sides. Peel off the hard shell.

Next time you babysit, ask the parents if you can serve their children pond scum. Watch the kids smile as you serve this sweet and fun creation. This pond scum is delicious!

POND SCUM

WHAT YOU NEED

•• Ingredients

1 (3-ounce) package instant
   green gelatin dessert
1 (4.5-ounce) package gummy fish
1 (4.5-ounce) package gummy bugs

•• Tools

mixing bowl   mixing spoon

small plastic cups

1 In a mixing bowl, prepare gelatin according to package directions. Allow gelatin to cool.

2 Using a large spoon, stir in gummy fish.

3 Place in refrigerator to cool and thicken for three to four hours.

4 When the gelatin is thick, add gummy bugs to the top so they sink in just a bit.

5 Dish out servings into clear plastic cups.

Food Fun Kids Will Love

Make food fun for kids, and you're sure to score more babysitting jobs.

- Slice snacks like apples and cheese into small pieces.

- Use cookie cutters to make sandwiches with unique shapes.

- Add a drop or two of food coloring to a glass of regular milk.

- Let kids help you cook. For the pond scum recipe, children could help stir the gelatin or add the gummy fish.

Camping trip rained out? A change of plans doesn't have to mean missing out on your favorite outdoor snack. These s'mores can be prepared in the kitchen.

DIFFICULTY LEVEL: ★ ★ ☆
SERVING SIZE: 6

INDOOR S'MORES

WHAT YOU NEED

●● *Ingredients*

1 (3-ounce) package instant
    chocolate pudding
1 box graham crackers
1 tub whipped topping
1 (10.5-ounce) package
    mini marshmallows

●● *Tools*

mixing bowl

mixing spoon

1 Using a mixing bowl and spoon, prepare pudding according to package directions. Set pudding aside.

2 Break a graham cracker into two squares.

3 Spoon about 1 tablespoon of pudding onto the center of each square.

4 Top s'more with whipped topping.

5 Top with about five mini marshmallows.

More S'mores, Please

The first recipe for s'mores was printed in the *Girl Scout Handbook* in 1927. The treat was an instant hit. Here's how you make the original:

1 Break a graham cracker into two squares.

2 Place about three squares or ¼ of a chocolate bar on one cracker half.

3 Toast a marshmallow on a long metal stick over a campfire.

4 Place the warm marshmallow on top of the chocolate and cover with the other graham cracker half.

It's a hot dog! No, it's PB & J with a banana! This little dish combines the best of three tasty treats. It hits the spot when you're starved for an after-school snack.

DIFFICULTY LEVEL: ★ ☆ ☆
SERVING SIZE: 1

BANANA DOGS

WHAT YOU NEED

•• *Ingredients*

peanut butter
hot dog buns
bananas
strawberry jelly
   (in a squeeze bottle)

•• *Tools*

butter knife

serving plate

1 Use a butter knife to spread peanut butter on the inside of a hot dog bun.

2 Peel a banana and put it in the bun.

3 Top the banana with jelly to look like ketchup.

24

Classic Combo

By the time they graduate high school, most Americans will have eaten 1,500 peanut butter and jelly sandwiches. That's a lot of PB & J! Try these variations, and you won't get bored:

• Mix honey or maple syrup into the peanut butter before spreading.

• Instead of jelly, use sliced apples and cinnamon.

• Add dried fruits and chopped nuts between the peanut butter and the jelly.

Need a sweet treat you can bring to a school party? Score an "A" with this dip. It's easy to make and tastes great too.

DIFFICULTY LEVEL: ★ ☆ ☆
SERVING SIZE: 6

BERRY YUMMY DIP

WHAT YOU NEED

●● *Ingredients*

2 cups prepared whipped
    topping, thawed
2 cups raspberry yogurt
1 cup frozen raspberries, thawed
1 cup fresh apples
1 cup fresh pears
1 cup fresh, whole strawberries

●● *Tools*

mixing bowl

mixing spoon

sharp knife

serving dish

1 Place whipped topping, yogurt, and raspberries in a mixing bowl. Using a large mixing spoon, mix ingredients until the raspberries are crushed and blended.

2 With a sharp knife, slice apples and pears into small pieces. Trim the leafy tops off the strawberries, if desired.

3 Arrange apples, pears, and strawberries on a serving dish with the bowl of yogurt mixture.

4 To eat, dip the fruit into the yogurt mixture.

Berry Good

Raspberries are usually red, but they can be black, purple, or gold too. Many local farms will let you pick your own fresh batch in the summer or fall.

TOOLS GLOSSARY

baking pan — a deep pan with sides that is used for baking

baking sheet — a flat metal tray used for baking

butter knife — an eating utensil often used to spread ingredients

cutting board — a wooden or plastic board used to protect other surfaces when cutting food

electric mixer — a food mixer powered by an electric motor

fondue forks — long forks with two prongs that are used to cook or dip food in a fondue pot

fondue pot — a pot that's specially made for fondue, often equipped with a heating element and spaces to hold fondue forks

measuring spoons — spoons with small deep scoops used to measure both wet and dry ingredients

microwave-safe mixing bowl — a bowl made of plastic or glass that is used to heat ingredients in a microwave

mixing bowl — a sturdy bowl used for mixing ingredients

mixing spoon — large spoon with wide circular end used to mix ingredients

oven mitt — large mitten made from heavy fabric used to protect hands when removing hot pans from the oven

pizza pan — circular pan that is usually made of metal that is used to bake pizzas

pot holder — thick, heavy fabric cut into a square or circle that is used to remove hot pans from an oven

rolling pin — a cylinder-shaped tool used to roll and flatten dough or other food

rubber scraper — a kitchen tool with a rubber paddle on the end, used for stirring and mixing

saucepan — a pot with a handle used for stovetop cooking

sharp knife — kitchen knife with long blade used to cut ingredients

vegetable peeler — a small tool with two blades used to remove peels from vegetables and fruits

GLOSSARY

crave (KRAYV) — to want something very much

cream (KREEM) — to mix ingredients until soft and smooth

fold (FOHLD) — to mix or add ingredients by gently turning the heavy ingredient over the light ingredient

invent (in-VENT) — to create a new thing or method

satisfy (SAT-iss-fye) — to please people by giving them enough

taste buds (TAYST BUDS) — groups of cells on the tongue that sense taste

variation (vair-ee-AY-shuhn) — something that is slightly different from another thing of the same type

Dalgleish, Sharon. *Snack Food.* Healthy Choices. North Mankato, Minn.: Smart Apple Media, 2007.

Ibbs, Katharine. *I Can Cook!* New York: DK, 2007.

Schaefer, Ted, and Lola Schaefer. *Snacks.* What's on Your Plate? Chicago: Raintree, 2006.

Wagner, Lisa. *Cool Sweets & Snacks to Eat: Easy Recipes for Kids to Cook.* Cool Cooking. Edina, Minn.: Abdo, 2007.

FactHound offers a safe, fun way to find Internet sites related to this book. All of the sites on FactHound have been researched by our staff.

Here's how:
1. Visit *www.facthound.com*
2. Choose your grade level.
3. Type in this book ID **1429613394** for age-appropriate sites. You may also browse subjects by clicking on letters, or by clicking on pictures and words.
4. Click on the **Fetch It** button.

FactHound will fetch the best sites for you!

ABOUT THE AUTHOR

When Heather E. Schwartz first began writing about cooking, she lived in an apartment so small, it didn't have a kitchen. She learned to be creative with a microwave and toaster. At the time, she wrote a column on cooking and entertaining for *Bridal Guide* magazine.

These days, Heather enjoys cooking with a real oven and stove at her home in Albany, N.Y., where she is a freelance writer. She recently contributed to a humorous cookbook for adults and also writes for publications like *National Geographic Kids*. She lives with her husband, Philip, and son, Nolan.

INDEX